Show-and-Tell Rose

written by Josie Lee
illustrated by Selina Alko

McGraw-Hill
School Division

New York   Farmington

Rose and her mom had just moved.
Now Rose would be going to a new
school. "You will make lots of
friends," said Mom.

"I hope so," said Rose. Mom drove
Rose to school. Then Mom went
home.

Rose wrote her name on a tag. Then
she found her desk and sat down.

Rose felt a bit sad because she
did not know anyone. But some of
the kids smiled at her. Rose
smiled back.

Mom picked up Rose after work.
Then they drove home together.
"Did you like your new class?"
Mom asked.

"I liked it a lot," said Rose.

"But we will have show-and-tell. I do not know what to bring."

"We can think about that," said Mom.

When they got home, Mom stopped
at the home next to theirs. "I want
you to meet a new friend," she said.

"This is Mr. Lin Chan," said Mom.

"It is good to know you," he said to Rose.

Lin asked Mom and Rose to eat
with him. He made some of the
dishes Rose liked best. Yum!

After they ate, Rose spoke to Mom
and Lin about show-and-tell. "I can't
buy something to bring to class,"
she said. "I have to make it."

Lin handed Rose a flower. "Where did you get this?" asked Rose.

"I made it," he said. "It's a rose, just like you! I can help you make one, too."

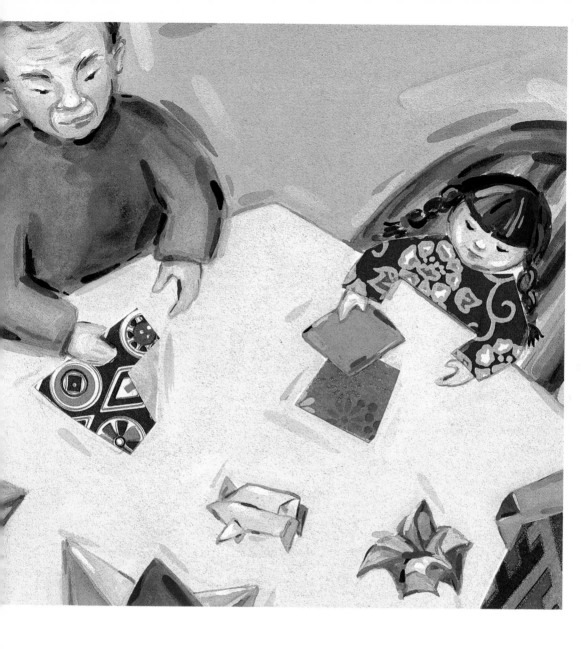

Lin showed Rose what to do. It
was a lot of work, but she became
good at it.

"Now I know what to take to class,"
Rose said.

Rose showed the class her rose.
Then she showed them how to
make it. "Thanks, Rose," said the
kids. "This is fun!"

Rose had made a new pal at
home. Now she had made pals in
class, too!